Dear Parents:

Congratulations! Your child is taking the first steps on an exciting journey. The destination? Independent reading!

STEP INTO READING® will help your child get there. The program offers five steps to reading success. Each step includes fun stories and colorful art or photographs. In addition to original fiction and books with favorite characters, there are Step into Reading Non-Fiction Readers, Phonics Readers and Boxed Sets, Sticker Readers, and Comic Readers—a complete literacy program with something to interest every child.

Learning to Read, Step by Step!

Ready to Read   Preschool–Kindergarten
• big type and easy words • rhyme and rhythm • picture clues
For children who know the alphabet and are eager to begin reading.

Reading with Help   Preschool–Grade 1
• basic vocabulary • short sentences • simple stories
For children who recognize familiar words and sound out new words with help.

Reading on Your Own   Grades 1–3
• engaging characters • easy-to-follow plots • popular topics
For children who are ready to read on their own.

Reading Paragraphs   Grades 2–3
• challenging vocabulary • short paragraphs • exciting stories
For newly independent readers who read simple sentences with confidence.

Ready for Chapters   Grades 2–4
• chapters • longer paragraphs • full-color art
For children who want to take the plunge into chapter books but still like colorful pictures.

STEP INTO READING® is designed to give every child a successful reading experience. The grade levels are only guides; children will progress through the steps at their own speed, developing confidence in their reading.

Remember, a lifetime love of reading starts with a single step!

New
+ Easy

Visit us on the Web!
StepIntoReading.com
randomhousekids.com

Educators and librarians, for a variety of teaching tools, visit us at RHTeachersLibrarians.com

ISBN 978-1-5247-1688-2 (trade) — ISBN 978-1-5247-1689-9 (lib. bdg.)

Printed in the United States of America   10 9 8 7 6 5 4 3 2 1

nickelodeon

Nella
THE PRINCESS KNIGHT

The BIG Birthday Surprise!

by Delphine Finnegan

based on the teleplay "A Really, Really Big Birthday
Surprise" by Jessica Silcock and Naomi Smith

illustrated by Susan Hall

Random House 🏠 New York

Nella, Clod, and Trinket
were setting up for
Garrett's birthday party.

The yummy food
was ready to eat.

King Dad's band
was warming up
and ready to rock.

There were piñatas,
bumper cars,
and lots of games.

Nella had a great idea.
She knew Garrett
missed his friend Bigor.

He had not seen
the dragon since
they were little.

It was time for
a knightly quest.
It was time to be . . .
a Princess Knight!

"Let's find Bigor,"
said Nella the
Princess Knight.

Nella, Clod, and Trinket
climbed Mount Dragon.

Falling rocks could
not stop them!

They ducked into a cave
and discovered . . .

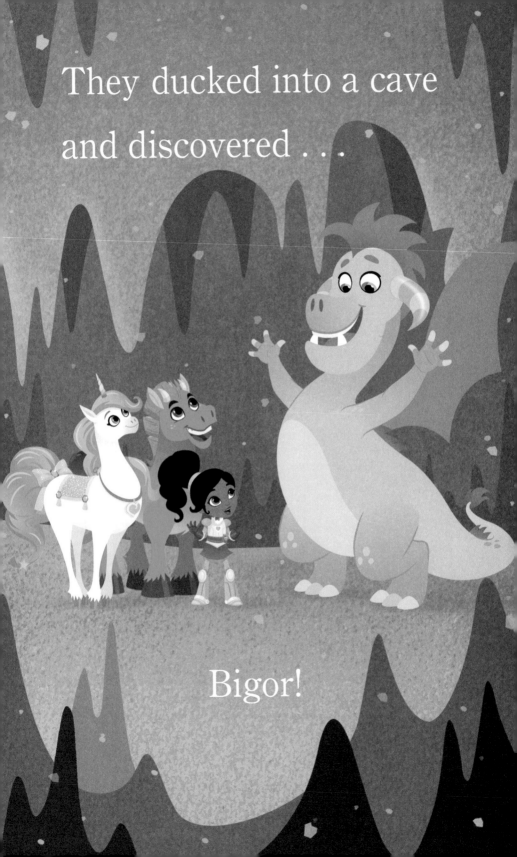

Bigor!

At the birthday party,
Clod covered
Garrett's eyes.

Surprise!

The two old friends

shared a big hug.

It was time to party.

Bigor swung

at the piñata.

He hit it far, far away.

Next, they drove
bumper cars.
Bigor was too big!
His car tipped over.

Soon it was time
for birthday cake.
Bigor helped Garrett
blow out the candles.

But the dragon's breath
set the cake and
streamers on fire!

Garrett was sad.
Bigor felt bad.
Nella's big surprise
was a big mess.

Nella had one more idea.
"Ready for the ride
of a lifetime?"
she asked the guests.

Nella and Bigor
surprised everyone
with a real dragon ride!

The whole party
flew over the kingdom.

Nella and her friends gave Garrett the best surprise and a really happy birthday!